The
Little Red Hen

RED FOX

The
Little Red Hen

·AN OLD STORY·

Margot Zemach

For My Little Red Hens

Abigail, Addie, Anat, Arisika, Aviva, Betty, Bobbi,
Carol, Charlotte, Clara, Ella, Elizabeth, Ethel, Frances,
Gina, Hannah, Helen, Jan, Jeanne, Kaethe, Kenar, Leigh,
Lois, Lotte, Marilyn, Mary, Mertis, Odette, Peggy, Penny,
Ruth, Sharon, Siri, Sonya, Sue, Toni, Tish, Ursula

A Red Fox Book

Published by Random House Children's Books
20 Vauxhall Bridge Road, London SW1V 2SA

A division of Random House UK Ltd
London Melbourne Sydney Auckland
Johannesburg and agencies throughout the world

3 5 7 9 10 8 6 4 2

First published by Farrar, Straus & Giroux, New York 1983
First published in Great Britain in 1985
Reprinted in 1991 by Hutchinson Children's Books

Red Fox edition 1994

Printed in Hong Kong

RANDOM HOUSE UK Limited Reg. No. 954009

ISBN 0 09 929001 4

Once upon a time a little red hen lived with her chicks in a small cottage. She worked hard to keep her family well fed. In the evenings, she sang while she worked.

One day when the little red hen was out walking with her friends, the goose, the cat, and the pig, she found a few grains of wheat.

"Who will plant this wheat?" she asked her friends, the goose, the cat, and the pig.

"Not I," said the goose.

"Not I," said the cat.

"Not I," said the pig.

"Then I'll do it myself," said the little red hen. And she did.

One morning the little red hen saw that the green wheat had sprouted.

"Oh, come and see the green wheat growing!" she called to her chicks.

All summer the wheat grew taller and taller. It turned from green to gold, and at last it was time for the wheat to be harvested.

"Who will harvest this wheat?" she asked her friends, the goose, the cat, and the pig.

"Not I," said the goose.

"Not I," said the cat.

"Not I," said the pig.

"Then I'll do it myself," said the little red hen. And she did.

At last the wheat was all cut down and it was time for it to be threshed.

"Who will thresh this wheat?" she asked her friends, the goose, the cat, and the pig.

"Not I," said the goose.

"Not I," said the cat.

"Not I," said the pig.

"Then I'll do it myself," said the little red hen. And she did.

At last the wheat was threshed, and the little red hen poured the golden grains into a large sack, ready to take to the mill to be ground into flour.

The next morning the little red hen asked her friends, the goose, the cat, and the pig: "Who will take this wheat to the mill to be ground into flour?"

"Not I," said the goose.

"Not I," said the cat.

"Not I," said the pig.

"Then I'll do it myself," said the little red hen. And she did.

The next day the little red hen asked her friends, the goose, the cat, and the pig: "Who will bake this flour into a lovely loaf of bread?"

"Not I," said the goose.

"Not I," said the cat.

"Not I," said the pig.

"Then I'll do it myself," said the little red hen. And she did.

At last the bread was baked and the little red hen called to her friends, the goose, the cat, and the pig: "Who will eat this lovely loaf of bread?"

"I will!" said the goose.

"I will!" said the cat.

"I will!" said the pig.

"Oh, no, you won't!" said the little red hen.

"I found the wheat and I planted it. I watched the wheat grow, and when it was time I harvested it and threshed it and took it to the mill to be ground into flour, and at last I've baked this lovely loaf of bread."

"Now," said the little red hen, "I'm going to eat it myself."
And she did!